Library of Congress Cataloging-in-Publication Data

Packard, Mary.
My messy room / by Mary Packard ; illustrated by Stephanie Britt.
p.   cm.
Summary: A stubborn young girl describes how she likes to keep her room very messy.
ISBN 0-590-90751-4
[1. Orderliness-Fiction.   2. Stories in rhyme.]   I.   Britt, Stephanie, ill.   II. Title.
PZ8.3.P125My   1993
[E]—dc20   92-36009
                                                                                          CIP
                                                                                          AC

24 23 22 21 20 19 18 17 16 15 14   6 7 8/9

Printed in the U.S.A.   24
First Scholastic printing, August 1993

MY MESSY ROOM

by Mary Packard
Illustrated by Stephanie Britt

My First Hello Reader!
With Flash Cards

SCHOLASTIC INC.

New York Toronto London Auckland Sydney

I like my room messy.

It's my room. So there!

I like paint
on my table.

I like socks on my chair.

I like books on my bed.

I like toys on my floor.

I like shirts
on my dresser.

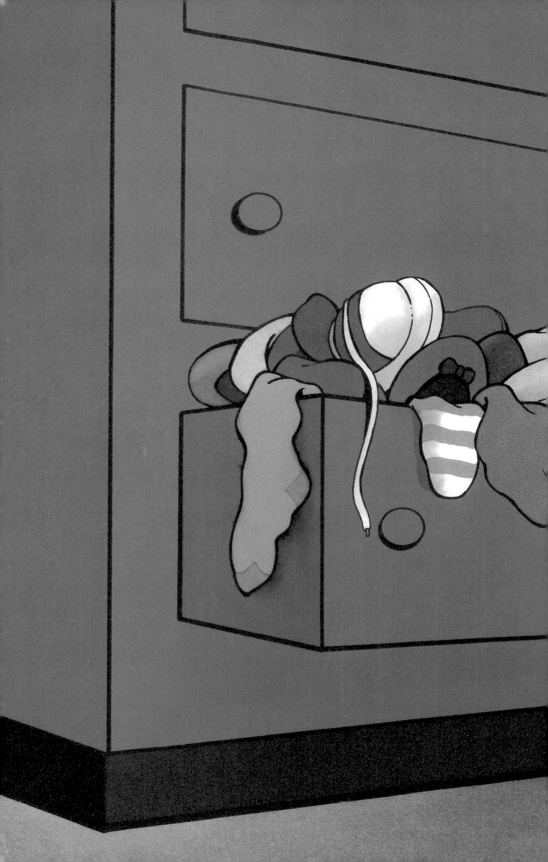

I like shoes
in my drawer.

I like my room messy.

I like it a lot.
I like it! I like it!

But Mommy does not!

A Very Messy Room

How many things can you find that begin with the letter **s**?

Think About It

The girl in this story feels glad when her room is a mess. Her mother does not. She feels mad!

What are some things that make you feel glad?

What makes you feel mad?

What makes you feel sad?

What makes you feel bad?

Messy Sentences

The words in these sentences got all mixed up.
Can you put them back in the right order?

messy my I like room

books my like bed I on

lot like I it a

Match Them Up

Use your fingers to match the words in the row on the left with the pictures of these words on the right.

socks

table

chair

shoes

paint

books

bed

Rhyme Time

The word *locks* rhymes with the word *socks*. Can you find words in the story that rhyme with these words?

tie

not

fair

boys

broom

door

Answers

(A Very Messy Room)
How many things did you find that began with the letter **s**? Some of these things are:

sailboat, sandwich, saw, saxophone, scarf, schoolbag, scissors, seat, sheet, shell, shelves, ship, shirt, shoe, shorts, shovel, skate, skateboard, sled, slipper, snowsuit, spoon, stamps, stapler, stereo, stethoscope, submarine, sunglasses, sweater

Did you find any other words?

(Think About It)
Answers will vary.

(Messy Sentences)
I like my room messy.
I like books on my bed.
I like it a lot.

(Rhyme Time)

tie / my	not / lot
fair / chair (there)	boys / toys
broom / room	door / floor (drawer)